First paperback edition 1994
Reprinted 1995, 1997, 2001
First Published 1985 in hardback by A&C Black (Publishers) Ltd
37 Soho Square, London W1D 3QZ

ISBN 0–7136–4084–7

A CIP catalogue record for this book is available from the British Library.

Acknowledgements
The author and publishers would like to thank Naomi Benscher for her help and
advice, Mr Wallace's class, Marsh Green Primary and, most especially, the
Rabin family whose help and co-operation made this book possible.

Filmset by August Filmsetting, Haydock, St Helens
Printed in Hong Kong by Imago

Sam's Passover

Lynne Hannigan

Photographs by Sally Fear

A & C Black · London

Hello! My name is Samuel Rabin.

This is me with my mum and dad and my two brothers, Daniel and Joseph.

My school is Marsh Green Primary. I'm in Mr Wallace's class.

Mr Wallace is waiting
for everyone to stop
wriggling and be quiet
so that he can tell us a
story.

The story is about
Moses, a great man who
lived a long time ago.
It's written in the
Old Testament of
the Bible.

I already know the story
because I'm Jewish and
the story is written on
big scrolls in our
synagogue.

3

'What's a scroll?' says Harcharan.
'What's a synagogue?' says Jay.

Mr Wallace says that we can all go to the synagogue and find out for ourselves.

We're going to the synagogue by coach.

When I go to synagogue with my family I wear a special hat, called a cuppal. Today I'm too shy to wear it, but some of the other boys bring hats.

Jay has a West Ham hat and Mathew has a balaclava. Harcharan wonders if his jura will count as a hat.

Rabbi Kraft shows us all the different things in the synagogue.

Everyone wants to see the scrolls. They're kept inside a special cupboard called the Ark.
Each one has a beautiful velvet and gold cover.

We're all trying to get a better look and Mathew nearly gets knocked over. Luckily, Rabbi Kraft isn't cross. A leaf gets broken off a big plant though.

The scrolls explain how Jewish people should live and they tell the stories of our religion. They are written in the Hebrew language. Each scroll is written by one person.

Rabbi Kraft shows us a plate and a silver cup.
They are only used once a year, at Pesach.

Pesach is the Hebrew word for Passover.
It's a special time for Jewish people like me.
We remember the time when the Jewish people
were slaves in Egypt and how God helped Moses
to set them free.

Harcharan, Darminder and Jack find some books about Passover and Rabbi Kraft says that we can keep one.

When it's time to go home, we all shout 'Shalom' to Rabbi Kraft. Shalom means peace, so you can use it for 'hello' or 'goodbye'.

When we get back to
school, Sheryl and
Jamie want to make
their own scrolls. They
write the story of
Passover on the scrolls
and roll them up like the
real ones.

Mr Wallace says that we
can send 'thank you'
cards to Rabbi Kraft.

We're writing 'Shalom' on our cards.
In Hebrew, it looks like this.

I'm learning Hebrew, so it's quite easy for me to
write my card.

Every Sunday I go to Hebrew classes.

Mrs Benscher teaches us to read and write in Hebrew and tells us stories about our religion.

Today we're practising the things we have to say and do at our Seder meal. The Seder is a family meal which we have at Passover.

I'm the youngest in my family so I have to ask some special questions and my dad has to answer them.

We practise the questions and then we put the matzos in their cover. Matzos are like big square biscuits. We always eat them at our Seder meal.

Mr Wallace says that we can lay the table for a Seder meal at school.

We're making our own matzo covers out of paper.

Patrick and James write matzo in Hebrew and make patterns on the covers.

It takes a long time because Patrick keeps eating the matzos.

We eat matzos at our Seder meal to help us remember the story of Passover. When the Jews escaped from Egypt they ate matzos because they didn't have enough time to bake bread.

My mum doesn't have to go to
work today. She's come to help us
do some cooking for Passover.
We're making coconut pyramids.

Mum shows us how to make the
mixture. Then we pat it into
pyramid shapes.

Lee and Telminder take our pyramids to the cookery room and put them in the oven. Everyone wants a taste.

We like to eat coconut pyramids at Pesach because they remind us of something. Can you guess what it is?

Yes – the pyramids which the Jews built when they were slaves.

After school we're going to buy some food for our Seder meal at home.

Mum wants to buy some chicken so we go to a Jewish butcher. There's a sign in the shop which says 'Kosher products sold here'.

Kosher is a Hebrew word. Mum says it means the kind of food which Jewish people should eat.

In the grocer's, Mum buys some matzos.
The packet says 'Kosher for Passover'.

There are special rules about Kosher food.
One rule is that a prayer must be said over the food.

Before Passover we have to clean the house and clear away old food.

Some people buy new knives and forks, too, but my mum has a special set just for Passover.

Mum gets the food ready to put on the Seder plate. Each thing on the plate helps us to remember the story of Passover.

There are bitter herbs to remind us of the hard life of the slaves in Egypt.

Charoseth is made from apples, almonds and wine. It reminds us of the clay which the slaves used to build with.

There are greens for springtime, a roasted egg and a lamb bone. Each one has a special place on the Seder plate.

As soon as it gets dark, we start our Seder meal.
Everyone is quiet until Joseph takes some bitter
herbs. He doesn't like them so he spits them out.
We all laugh.

Every year at the Seder meal I have to ask these questions. 'Why is this night different from all other nights and why do we have special things like bitter herbs and matzos?'

My dad answers the questions by telling the story of Passover and how the Jews escaped from Egypt.

Now at Passover, we think about other people who are not free. We pray for them and perhaps try to help them.

More about Passover

The story of Passover is more than 3 000 years old. If you want to find out more about it, try reading the whole story for yourself or ask someone to read it to you. It's written in the Old Testament of the Bible. The story is also in some of the books shown on this page.

Here is a *very* short outline of the story.

Long, long ago the Israelites were slaves in Egypt. They had to work very hard building cities and palaces for Pharaoh, the King of Egypt, and they were treated very cruelly.

Moses, the leader of the Israelites, asked Pharaoh to let his people go. But Pharaoh kept saying no.

God sent ten plagues to make Pharaoh change his mind. One plague was millions of frogs. The last plague was death. The oldest boy in every Egyptian family died, but the houses of the Israelites were 'passed over' and their children did not die. The Pharaoh's own son died and he was so upset that he let Moses lead the Israelites out of Egypt.

You might not have heard some of the words in this book. This is how they are usually pronounced.

Synagogue	*sinagog*
Pesach	*Paysuck*
Seder	*Sayder*
Rabbi	*Rab-eye*
Charoseth	*Haroset*

Things to do

1. Try to find out more about:
The burning bush.
The ten plagues.
How the Israelites crossed the Red Sea.

2. A synagogue is a place where Jewish people go to pray. Do you and your family have a special place where you pray? Is it a gurdwara, a church, a mosque, a special place in your house, or somewhere else? Compare stories with your friends.

3. Make a poster with the Hebrew word 'Shalom'. Shalom means peace. On your poster, draw a picture about peace.

4. Passover is a Spring festival and there are some things on the Seder plate which remind us of Spring. Can you think of any other festivals around the world which celebrate Spring? What about Easter or Holi? Try to find out more about Spring festivals and make a book about them.

5. At Passover, an extra cup is put on the Seder table. It's called the Cup of Elijah. Try to find out more about it.

6. Make a collection of different kinds of bread. Don't forget matzo, roti, croissant and pitta. How many other kinds can you find?

Books to read

Old Testament (Exodus)
Moses and the flight from Egypt, *by D. Craig* (Macdonald)
The Jewish World, *by Rabbi Douglas Charing* (Macdonald)
Matza and Bitter Herbs, *by Clive Lawton* (Hamish Hamilton)
Shimon, Leah and Benjamin, *by C. Knapp* (Black)